Craftily EVER AFTER

-- DIY Pet Shop --

By Martha Maker   Illustrated by Xindi Yan

LITTLE SIMON
New York London Toronto Sydney New Delhi

LITTLE SIMON

An imprint of Simon & Schuster Children's Publishing Division
1230 Avenue of the Americas, New York, New York 10020
First Little Simon paperback edition November 2018
Copyright © 2018 by Simon & Schuster, Inc.
All rights reserved, including the right of reproduction in whole or in part in any form.
LITTLE SIMON is a registered trademark of Simon & Schuster, Inc.,
and associated colophon is a trademark of Simon & Schuster, Inc.
For information about special discounts for bulk purchases, please contact Simon & Schuster
Special Sales at 1-866-506-1949 or business@simonandschuster.com.
The Simon & Schuster Speakers Bureau can bring authors to your live event.
For more information or to book an event contact the Simon & Schuster Speakers Bureau at
1-866-248-3049 or visit our website at www.simonspeakers.com.
Designed by Laura Roode
The text of this book was set in Caecilia.
Manufactured in the United States of America 1018 MTN
2 4 6 8 10 9 7 5 3 1
Cataloging-in-Publication Data is available for this title from the Library of Congress.
ISBN 978-1-5344-2900-0 (hc)
ISBN 978-1-5344-2899-7 (pbk)
ISBN 978-1-5344-2901-7 (eBook)

CONTENTS

CHAPTER 1

Knot a Problem

Bella Diaz was in the craft clubhouse—formerly known as the old shack in her backyard—waiting for her three best friends to arrive. It was Saturday afternoon. As often as possible, and especially on weekends, the foursome met up at the clubhouse to do craft projects together.

Knock, knock-knock, knock!

Bella jumped to her feet at the sound of the familiar knock. But when she opened the door, she did not see a familiar face. All she could see were sequined sneakers, bright purple leggings, and two hands carrying a towering pile of fabric pieces.

"Maddie?" Bella guessed.

"How'd you know?" The sneakers shuffled forward, and the giant pile of material landed with a soft *thump* on the big worktable. Maddie Wilson's trademark grin came into view.

"Lucky guess," said Bella, smiling back. Maddie was the stylish seamstress of the bunch, and since her mother was a fashion designer, she often got her mom's leftover scraps.

"Very cool," Bella added. "But what are all these scraps for?"

"My mom just finished creating an entire line of fleece jackets, so she gave me the leftover material.  It's so cuddly and soft. I thought we could make knotted blankets."

"What's a knotted blanket?" asked Emily Adams as she and Sam Sharma entered the clubhouse. Now all four friends were there.

"This!" Maddie showed them a pattern. "See? You cut out a square at each corner, and then you cut fringe all the way around. After that you line up the two pieces of cloth and knot the fringe together. Or braid them, if you prefer. There are lots of ways to do it."

The four friends were game, so they each selected fabric pieces and quickly got to work.

Or tried to.

"This is harder than it looks," said Emily.

Sam nodded. "My knots are *not* holding."

Bella came over to take a look. "Do either of you know how to make a square knot?"

They didn't, but they learned quickly when Bella showed them a how-to video on her computer. "See? *Knot* a problem," she joked.

Everyone laughed.

Before long, all four friends were working away, knotting and braiding the fringes on their blankets in different patterns.

"These are cool," said Sam. "What are we going to do with them when we're done?"

"I'm not sure," admitted Maddie. "They're pretty small. I guess we could leave an opening and put stuffing between the two layers? That would make them into pillows."

"They'd make cute dog beds, too," said Emily.

"Ohh, that reminds me . . . ,"
said Sam. "It's my turn to take Bibi
out. If I'm late, it will be trouble."

"Sam, you are so lucky," said
Emily. "I wish I could have a dog,
but my parents think it's too much
work."

"Well, they're kind of right," said
Sam.

"Hey, whose side are you on?" said Emily, jabbing Sam's arm playfully.

"I'm just saying, it's totally worth it, but it is a lot of responsibility and a lot of work," Sam said with a smile.

Emily nodded, but the only part she heard loud and clear was: "totally worth it."

Puppy Practice

The next day Emily woke up still thinking about dogs. She *really* wanted one. But how could she convince her parents? She remembered what Sam said about it being a big responsibility. What if . . . ? That was it! She had an idea!

Later that morning, Emily called Sam and excitedly explained her plan.

"If I pitch in more at home, my parents will see how responsible I am," she said. "Then they couldn't possibly say no to a dog. I'll take out the garbage and unload the dish-washer without being asked, set the table, and—"

"Okay, but how will you show them you know how to care for a dog?" asked Sam.

"Well, I could . . ." Emily hadn't thought about that.

"You could practice by helping me with Bibi," suggested Sam.

"Would your parents let me?"

"Of course!"

On Monday, Emily went to Sam's house after school. Bibi met them at the door, jumping around and barking excitedly.

"Hand me the leash, quick!" said Sam.

"What's the rush?" asked Emily.

"She's still a puppy," said Sam, trying to grab Bibi while she wiggled just out of reach. "So, when she gets excited, she—"

"Oops!" said Emily, noticing a puddle.

"Aw, Bibi," said Sam.

"You take her out. I'll wipe it up," offered Emily.

While Sam took Bibi around the block, Emily wiped up the mess. It wasn't fun, but it made her feel like a real dog owner. And when Sam got back, Emily got to do the *really* fun part: playing with Bibi and teaching her tricks.

That night Emily set and cleared the table, loaded the dishwasher, and took out the trash and the recycling. The next morning she set her alarm for a half hour before she usually got up, to practice for when she had a dog of her own to walk. Since she was up early anyway, she decided to make coffee for her parents. She'd seen her dad do it enough times, though she still sort of had to wing it.

When her father came downstairs, he raised an eyebrow.

"You made coffee?" he asked.

"Yup!" said Emily proudly. "I'm doing extra chores and getting up early and learning dog care from Sam. You know, just in case we ever decide to get a dog."

All week long Emily tried to think of chores and jobs she could do to demonstrate how responsible she was. She even skipped going to the craft clubhouse with her friends. She figured that if she had a real dog, it would have to take priority.

On Friday morning she noticed a tiny paper animal on her friends'

desks. A purple monkey, a green swan, and a yellow frog.

"Where did you guys get those?" she asked Sam.

"We made them at the club-house yesterday!" he replied.

Emily felt a twinge of sadness that she'd missed out on the fun. But she reminded herself what Sam had said about caring for a dog: It's hard work, but it's worth it.

By dinnertime that night Emily was feeling tired from getting up early all week and doing chores every afternoon. At the table, she closed her eyes to rest them, just for a moment.

Crash!

Emily's eyes flew open. She jumped up at the sudden feeling

of something cold and damp. *Oh no!* She had dozed off and knocked over her glass of milk. And what was worse—the glass had shattered on the floor.

Tears welled in Emily's eyes. "I'm so s-sorry!" she said. "I'll clean it up!" She couldn't believe she had been so clumsy. After all her hard work being responsible all week, now she was ruining everything.

"Emily, it's okay," said her mom gently. "Your dad and I have noticed all the work you've been doing to take care of things around the house. And we really appreciate it."

"But you don't have to get carried away," said her dad. "There are bound to be accidents and messes from time to time. That's just the way it is with a new puppy."

"With a . . . what?" Emily looked at him, confused.

"Hang on," said Emily's mom, smiling. "We're not getting a dog quite yet. But your dad and I have been impressed with how hard you've been working to prove you're ready. So we decided it might be a good time for you to volunteer at our local animal shelter if you'd like. That way you'll learn more about pet care. And then, if the right dog comes along, we can consider it."

"Really?!" Emily asked. Her mom
and dad nodded.

Emily couldn't believe it. Her
plan had worked . . . almost!

CHAPTER
3

Training Day

On Saturday morning Emily was the first one downstairs. She tried to be patient, but waiting was even worse than taking out the garbage.

Finally, it was time to go to the shelter. Emily's mom had already explained that Emily wasn't old enough to volunteer on her own, but she could participate in a "shelter

assistant" program with a parent. And Emily's mom was willing to join her!

"Nice to meet you, Emily," said the man who greeted them at the shelter. "I'm Dave, and your mom tells me you're really responsible.

Today's volunteer training session will start soon. For now, why don't you go look around."

Emily made a beeline for the door marked DOGS FOR ADOPTION. On the other side she found a long hallway lined with separate

kennels holding one or two dogs.
The kennels had glass on one side,
and almost all the dogs ran up to
the glass when they saw Emily.

Emily caught sight of an especially cute dog with long floppy ears.

"Hi, sweetie," she said, leaning in toward the kennel.

"Ahhh-ahhh-ahhh-chooo!"

The dog jumped back in surprise.

Emily stepped away, a little embarrassed by her loud sneeze. Then she noticed another cute dog. This one was big, jet-black, and shaggy. She went over to take a look.

She felt like she might sneeze
again, but she managed not to.

She rubbed her
eyes. She decided to
go get a tissue and
some water. Then
she joined her mom in
the waiting room. There were a few
other kids and parents there too.

Just then Dave came in and addressed the group. "I know you're all eager to meet our adorable shelter residents. They're excited to meet you, too."

Emily smiled. The two dogs she'd already met were definitely excited to see her.

"But first," Dave continued, "we need to go over the rules and expectations we have for all our volunteers. We'll start by watching a short video."

Emily enjoyed the training session. There was a lot to learn, but the training made her feel like an important member of the shelter team. According to Dave, it was up to all of them to care for the animals while the animals waited for their "forever family."

I hope my family can be a dog's "forever family," Emily thought as she left the shelter at the end of the day. She sneezed again. But first, I hope I'm not getting sick!

CHAPTER 4

A Dog Named Woody

The next morning Emily was happy to discover that she didn't feel sick anymore. She bounced out of bed and got dressed in a hurry, tossing her brand-new SHELTER VOLUNTEER T-shirt in her backpack. Now she'd be ready to go after school.

The school day went slower than it had ever gone before. At lunch,

Emily's friends were all talking about their crafting plans for that afternoon.

Emily was sorry she was going to miss out *again*, but she was also really excited to return to the shelter.

After school Emily and her mom went straight there.

"Let's start by taking a tour of the whole shelter," Dave suggested to the group. "We'll start in the cat complex."

Emily and her mom followed Dave. As soon as he opened the door, they heard a chorus of *meows*.

"Wow," said Emily. There were cats in kennels, but many of the cats were exploring the common space. Rising almost to the ceiling were wooden and carpeted climbing towers, which were being scaled by some of the more curious cats.

Emily loved to design and build things. She wanted to spend time with the dogs, but maybe she could also volunteer to build some more climbing towers for the shelter!

Emily began to speak, but instead of words—"*ah-ah-ah-chooooo!*"—a sneeze came out.

Oh no. Not those pesky sneezes again!

Emily swallowed quickly and tried again. "It's totally awesome here. It's really—*ah-choo! Ah-choo!*"

Dave gave Emily a funny look.

"On second thought, let's go back to the front desk," he said. "There's some office work I could really use your help with. And we'll find tasks for the rest of you too!" he told the group.

Emily smiled, trying to be agreeable. But all she could think was: *Me and my big sneezes! He's probably worried I'm going to get the cats sick or something.*

Emily and her mom spent the rest of the afternoon stuffing envelopes, making copies of a handout for a puppy kindergarten class, and folding donated towels. Emily knew all these tasks were important, but she missed the animals.

Looking out the office window into the shelter's outdoor play yard, Emily saw a girl walking a shelter dog on a leash. Two adults were with her, and Emily saw them nod. Then the girl knelt and hugged the dog.

Emily felt a pang of jealousy. She closed her eyes and pictured her perfect dog, with bright shining eyes, soft-as-velvet fur, a wagging tail, and kisses to spare.

Just then an elderly man walked into the shelter with an adorable fluffy dog that reminded Emily of Sam's dog, Bibi. But this one had shiny brown fur. The man came up to the desk and spoke to Dave.

Emily strained to hear what the man was saying. She caught only bits and pieces. She heard the man say something about his neighbors moving and having to give up their

dog, and how he knew this would be the best place for the dog since he couldn't take care of it. Then she clearly heard him say that the dog's name was Woody.

Emily saw Dave hold out his hand for the dog to sniff.

Then she was pretty sure she heard Dave say, "Dogs like this don't come in very often. We'll find

Woody a good home in no time."

Dogs like this don't come in often? What did that mean? Emily started to wander over to the front desk, hoping to take a closer look. But before she could, Dave whisked the dog away to the examination room so the shelter veterinarians could make sure he was healthy.

Emily tried not to get her hopes up, but she couldn't help feeling like there was something special about Woody.

Ah-Ah-Ah Chooooo!

The next afternoon, something came up at Emily's mom's office, so she couldn't take Emily to the shelter. Instead, Emily was happy enough to go to the craft clubhouse with her friends.

"Check it out," said Bella. "We learned to do a whole bunch of new origami folds yesterday. I'll show you the website with the instructions. It was super-easy!"

"Maybe for you," said Maddie. "Everything I made came out looking like a swan. Fat swan, skinny swan, long-necked swan, giant swan . . ."

"Maddie!" said Bella. "You're being too hard on yourself. Anyone can see that's a parrot, a butterfly, a rose, and, um, uh . . . a giant swan?"

"I told you so!" Maddie laughed. "It's okay. Luckily, I have other talents."

"Are there instructions for folding a dog?" asked Emily.

"Sure! All kinds of dogs," said Bella excitedly. "Here, let me show you."

Emily joined Bella at the computer. Sure enough, the screen was soon filled with all sorts of dogs.

Emily was so captivated by the possibilities that she didn't hear the clubhouse door open. "Wow!" she said. "I want to make them—*ah-ah-ah-ah-choo!*"

"My swans!" said Maddie, div-
ing forward as Emily's sneeze sent
the origami creations sailing off the
table.

"I'm so sorry!" said Emily, ducking down and meeting Maddie on the floor to gather up the origami creatures.

Just then Emily noticed she was face-to-face with Sam's bright yellow sneakers. As well as twelve furry paws!

"Woof! Woof! Woof!" barked all three dogs.

"Bibi! Riley! Rocky! Stop!" yelled Sam, trying to get them under control.

"What in the world?" said Bella. "Sam, did you get two more dogs?"

"No. Riley and Rocky belong to my cousins," explained Sam. "They're out of town, so we agreed to watch their dogs. My mom asked me to get them out of the house so she could vacuum—they're shedding all over the furniture. Bibi doesn't shed, so we've never had to deal with this!"

Emily wanted to tell Sam about volunteering at the shelter. But when she opened her mouth, all that came out was *"ah-choo!"*

"Sorry!" said Emily, grabbing a handful of tissues. "I must be getting a cold or something. I should probably go home before I get everyone sick."

Emily grabbed her backpack and ducked out the door, giving all three dogs quick hi-and-bye pats as she passed Sam.

"Ah-choo! Ah-choo! Ah-CHOO!"

And with that, Emily sneezed herself out the door.

CHAPTER
6

Diagnosis: Disaster

"I don't feel sick anymore," said Emily at breakfast the next morning. "I haven't sneezed since yesterday afternoon, honest!"

She hoped this would convince her mom to let her go to the shelter today. Instead, her mom responded, "Good! But we'll go see Dr. Martin after school. Just to be sure."

The nice thing about Dr. Martin was that she took the time to ask good questions and really listen to the answers. Emily was planning to become an engineer or an architect, but Dr. Martin made Emily feel like it might be cool to be a doctor, too. Or maybe a veterinarian!

"So, when did you first notice the sneezing?" asked Dr. Martin. "And did you have any other symptoms? Itchy eyes? A scratchy throat?"

Emily answered all of Dr. Martin's questions, then let Dr. Martin examine her eyes, ears, throat, and nose.

"Everything looks okay," said Dr. Martin. "One more question, Emily. When did you notice that the symptoms had gone away?"

"Well, actually, it happened a few times," replied Emily. "Twice, when I went home from volunteering at the animal shelter. And yesterday I felt sick at the craft clubhouse, but then I was fine this morning."

"There wouldn't happen to be any pets at the craft clubhouse, would there?"

"No," said Emily. "Just me and my friends. Oh, wait. Yesterday Sam brought three dogs with him. You don't think I got them sick, do you?"

"Nope," said Dr. Martin. "In fact, I don't think you're sick at all."

"See!" said Emily, turning to her mom. "I told you I wasn't sick." She turned back to Dr. Martin. "So, I can go back to volunteering tomorrow, right?"

"Well, there's a little problem," said Dr. Martin. "Emily, I think I know why you've been sneezing and having itchy eyes when you're around dogs and cats."

"You do?"

Dr. Martin nodded. Then she said four words Emily didn't want to hear:

"I think you're allergic."

Paper Pooches

"We're glad you're here," said Bella the next afternoon, when Emily arrived at the craft clubhouse.

Maddie and Sam nodded in agreement. Emily knew they were trying to be supportive. She'd told them what Dr. Martin said about her allergies.

"Thanks," said Emily. "I just wish

I could be at the animal shelter too. Now, not only is it looking like I won't be able to get a dog, but I can't even be near them."

"I'm so sorry," said Maddie sympathetically. "This isn't the same thing, but I know one kind of dog you *can* be around. An origami dog!"

"Good idea!" said Bella. "Emily, you can fold all the dogs you want and none of them will make you sneeze."

They pulled out the origami paper and got to work. The first

few dogs they folded were pretty rough, but with practice they got better. Emily "walked" her folded paper dog—just like a real dog.

Except it wasn't a real dog. It was just a folded piece of paper. You couldn't cuddle an origami dog.

It wouldn't lick your face or wag its tail with excitement when you came home.

Emily sighed. Her thoughts went back to the shelter. She wondered if that sweet dog Woody had found *his* forever family yet.

CHAPTER 8

A Surprising Discovery

The next morning at school, Emily was still feeling down. Though she brightened up when her teacher, Ms. Gibbons, invited the class to line up for library time. Emily loved to read.

She decided to look for a book on dog breeds. If she couldn't be around dogs, she could at least

read about them. Sure enough, she
found a heavy nonfiction book with
photographs and detailed information. She turned to the index and
looked under P.

Papillon . . . Pekingese . . . Pointer . . .
Pomeranian . . . Poodle!

The book had photographs of a variety of poodles. Emily read about their history, temperament, size, and color variations. She was about to turn the page when she noticed something.

"'Poodles are hypoallergenic,'" she read aloud.

"Hypoallergenic" was a new word for Emily, so she looked it up. Her heart began to beat faster when she found the definition.

Hypoallergenic: not likely to trigger an allergic reaction.

She went on to read:

While no dog is 100 percent hypoallergenic, there are a variety of breeds that do well with those suffering from allergies. These dogs have a non-shedding

coat that produces less dander.
Dander, which is attached to
pet hair, is what causes most pet
allergies in humans.

Emily gasped. Maybe there was still hope. Maybe . . . she could get a dog after all!

High Hopes

After school Emily excitedly reported her findings to her mom. She pulled out the dog breed book she'd borrowed from the library to prove that her information was accurate.

"And I talked to Sam, and we realized that the reason I never had a problem around his dog is because *she's* hypoallergenic!" Emily added.

"Hmm," said her mom. "I suppose if there was a dog at the shelter that happened to be hypoallergenic . . ."

Emily clasped her hands with excitement.

"But we don't know if there are any," her mom continued. "And

I would hate for you to get your hopes up only to find that your allergies are too severe for this to work."

"I won't get my hopes up!" promised Emily, silently adding: *Any more than they are already.*

At home, Emily's mom gave her the phone number for the shelter. She hadn't told them that she wouldn't be able to volunteer there anymore. So she dialed the number to tell Dave. And she had another question for him too.

"I'm so sorry to hear about your allergies!" Dave said sincerely when he heard the news.

"Me too," said Emily. "And . . . uh . . . I was also wondering about something else," she said, her heart pounding. "Do you happen to have any hypoallergenic dogs at the shelter right now?"

There was a pause at the other end of the line. She heard some papers rustling.

"Aha!" Dave finally said. "Emily, you're in luck. There's a dog named Woody here. . . . Hello?"

In her excitement, Emily had dropped the phone. She scooped it up from the ground. "Hi. Sorry!" she said. "I remember Woody! He was brought in the last day I volunteered there, and he seemed *sooo* sweet."

"He is so sweet," Dave said. "And I told the man who brought him in that dogs like that don't come in often, because I could tell immediately that he was a hypoallergenic mix of breeds."

Ah, so that's what that meant, thought Emily. "Could I . . . come meet Woody?" Emily asked nervously.

"Of course! Just let me know

when, and I'll get him ready," Dave told her.

When Emily hung up the phone, she felt happier than ever. She couldn't believe it. She'd felt there was something special about Woody, and maybe that was it. Maybe he was meant for her!

Lucky Dog!

A few days later, Emily could barely contain her excitement. She was on her way to the shelter.

When they pulled into the parking lot, Emily took some deep breaths and reminded herself to stay calm. If it turned out Woody wasn't the right dog for her family, she'd be disappointed, but she knew she'd be okay.

Dave welcomed Emily and her parents into the shelter and then brought them to an office, where he went over some guidelines about what to do when meeting a dog for the first time. Then he led them into the backyard—where Emily had seen the little girl playing with the dog.

Emily did as Dave had told her. She walked into the yard and didn't make eye contact with Woody— which was so hard because he was so cute! Then she waited. After about a minute, Woody slowly approached Emily. She held out her hand, and he sniffed it . . . and then licked it! Emily giggled.

Dave had told Emily and her parents the commands that Woody already knew—sit, stay, and roll over. And he'd told them to give Woody those commands to test his reaction. Emily's parents let her try first.

"Sit," she told Woody. The dog cocked his head and then sat!

"Stay," she said as she backed away, and Woody stood as still as a statue.

"Roll over!" Emily commanded, and Woody gave a playful bark and then rolled over on the ground.

"Good boy!" Emily said excitedly, and Woody came over. She knelt down, and he started licking her face. She laughed—and couldn't *stop* laughing, which only made Woody want to lick her more!

And maybe best of all . . . no sneezes!

Emily and her parents spent an hour with Woody, going through all the things Dave had told them to do.

And when the hour was up, Emily was sure of it. Woody was her dog.

Emily's family went back the

next day to spend more time with Woody. And the next day. And the next day. Emily's parents and the shelter wanted to be sure that it was the right match.

And it was. Because a few days later, Emily and her parents pulled up to the shelter. But Emily wasn't just excited to be bringing Woody home.

When she had told her friends the news, it had reminded Maddie that

they had all those mini blankets. Maddie suggested they stuff the blankets to *actually* make dog beds, and that's exactly what the four friends had done. In the trunk of Emily's parents' car, there was a big bag with all the beds inside.

"Wow," said Dave when Emily presented him with the beds. "This is so generous of you and your friends. Woody is one lucky dog!"

Emily beamed.

That night, at home with Woody, Emily served him the food the shelter had given them to start. Then she took him for a walk around the block. When they came back, Woody went right over to his bed and lay down. Emily had saved one of the knotted-blanket beds for him, and he certainly seemed to like it. Emily reached into her pocket to give him a treat, but she pulled something else out instead. It was her origami dog!

She smiled. Now she could play
with an origami dog *and* a real dog.
Her very own real dog!

How to Make . . .

An Origami Dog

What you need:

1 piece of square origami paper
Pen or marker

Start with your square
piece of origami paper.
Place it down so it looks
like a diamond.

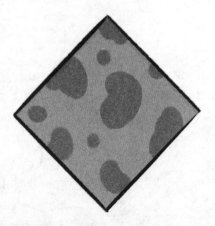

Fold the square in half by folding the top corner to the bottom corner. Now you have a triangle.

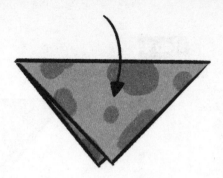

Fold the triangle in half by folding the left corner to the right corner.

Unfold the last fold.

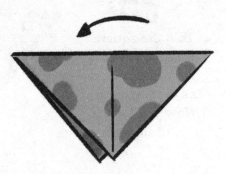

Step 5: Fold the left corner down to make the dog's left ear, and fold the right corner down to make the dog's right ear.

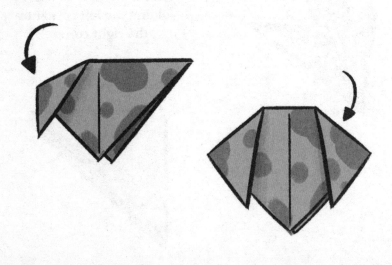

Fold the bottom corner up to make the dog's nose.

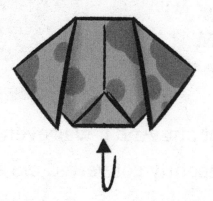

Use your pen or marker to draw the dog's face!

Woof, woof!

Here's a sneak peek at the next Craftily Ever After book!

It was *hot* out. And it was even hotter in the recently converted old shed—now known as the craft clubhouse—in Bella Diaz's backyard. Bella and her three best friends were in there working on different craft projects. They'd propped the doors open to catch the occasional breeze.

Despite the heat, the four friends were having fun. Sam Sharma was pinning up his latest sketches and planning his next painting. Maddie Wilson was sewing sequins onto the sleeves of a dress she was making. Bella was writing code for a new video game. And Emily Adams had just finished sawing a piece of wood.

"Hey, are we out of sandpaper?" asked Emily after she checked the supply shelves.

Bella shrugged. "I don't usually use sandpaper when I'm coding." She laughed. "So I don't know. Are we out of it?"

"Looks like it. I need to sand

the puppy stepladder I'm making." Emily showed her new project to her friends. "See? Otherwise Woody will try to climb onto my bed and end up with splinters in all four paws!"

"Woof!" said Sam. "I guess we need to pick up some sandpaper. In the meantime, want to grab a paintbrush and help me?"

"Sure," said Emily. But when she looked in the paint supply area, she called out, "We're out of paint, too."

"You guys can always sew with me," called Maddie. "Check it out!

This is the dress I'm going to wear to my cousin's wedding!"

"Did you say *dress*?" asked Bella. "I think you mean shirt."

Sure enough, the garment ended at Maddie's waist.

"It's fine," said Maddie, rummaging through the sewing supplies. "I'll just piece together some more fabric and . . . Oh no! I thought we had plenty of this fabric. I can't go to the wedding with half a dress!"

"Want me to start a shopping list?" suggested Bella, opening a new window on her computer. "Paint, sandpaper, fabric . . . Anything else?"

"Yes," said Emily, looking at the craft clubhouse's mostly empty storage shelves. "We're running low on almost everything."

"What are we going to do?" asked Sam. "I can't paint without paint."

"And I can't sew without fabric," added Maddie.

"Yeah, wood might grow on trees, but sandpaper sure doesn't," joked Emily.

Bella laughed. "Well, how about we figure out how to get more supplies?"